To Sue, my number one fan

Balzer + Bray is an imprint of HarperCollins Publishers.

The Digger and the Dark
Copyright © 2024 by Joseph Kuefler
All rights reserved. Manufactured in Italy.
No part of this book may be used or reproduced in any manner whatsoever
without written permission except in the case of brief quotations embodied in
critical articles and reviews. For information address HarperCollins Children's
Books, a division of HarperCollins Publishers, 195 Broadway, New York, NY 10007.
www.harpercollinschildrens.com

Library of Congress Control Number: 2023944493
ISBN 978-0-06-323793-3

Typography by Joseph Kuefler and Dana Fritts
24 25 26 27 28   RTLO   10 9 8 7 6 5 4 3 2 1

First Edition

THE DIGGER AND (THE DARK

JOSEPH KUEFLER

squeak squeak

BALZER + BRAY
An Imprint of HarperCollinsPublishers

It was getting late,
and Digger and the crew
were still hard at work.

"My stripes aren't straight,"
said Stripes.

"I stacked the wrong stuff,"
said Hoist.

"It is too dark to build," said Digger. "Let's finish in the morning."

The other big trucks agreed.

So they readied themselves for bed.

They washed.

They brushed.

They snuggled.

"Goodnight," said Digger.
"Sleep tight," said Sweeps.

Before the big trucks could fall asleep . . .

a pair of raccoons appeared.

"They're banging in my bucket," said Skid.

"They're hanging on my hook," said Crane.

"They're tickling my tanks," said Stripes.

"Squeak squeak," said the raccoons.

"We will play with you," said Digger.
"But only for a minute."

So the big trucks raced.

They bounced.

They played until the sun came up.

The next morning, the raccoons went to bed. The big trucks went back to work.

"Those raccoons wore me out," said Digger. Claw agreed.

But the big trucks
had work to do.

When evening came,
they sipped

and went

and read.

"I'm exhausted," said Crane.
"Me too," said Sweeps.

"Shh," said Digger. "Time for bed."

But just as the big trucks were
about to fall asleep . . .

the raccoons returned.

"Squeak squeak,"
said the raccoons.

"Absolutely not!" said Crane.
"It's too late for a snack."
The other big trucks agreed.

But Digger did not.
"You do look hungry," said Digger.
"Just a tiny snack."

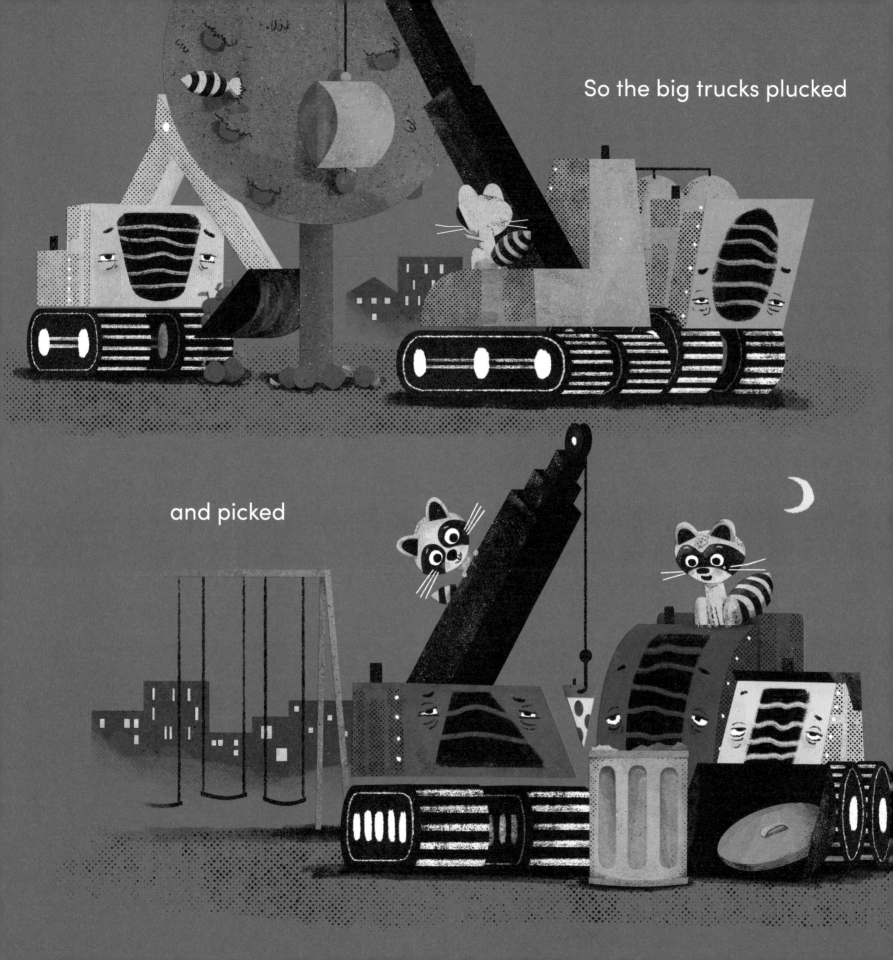

So the big trucks plucked

and picked

and fed their furry friends
all night long.

squeak squeak squeak squeak squeak squeak

Every evening, the raccoons returned.

For a chat.

For a scratch.

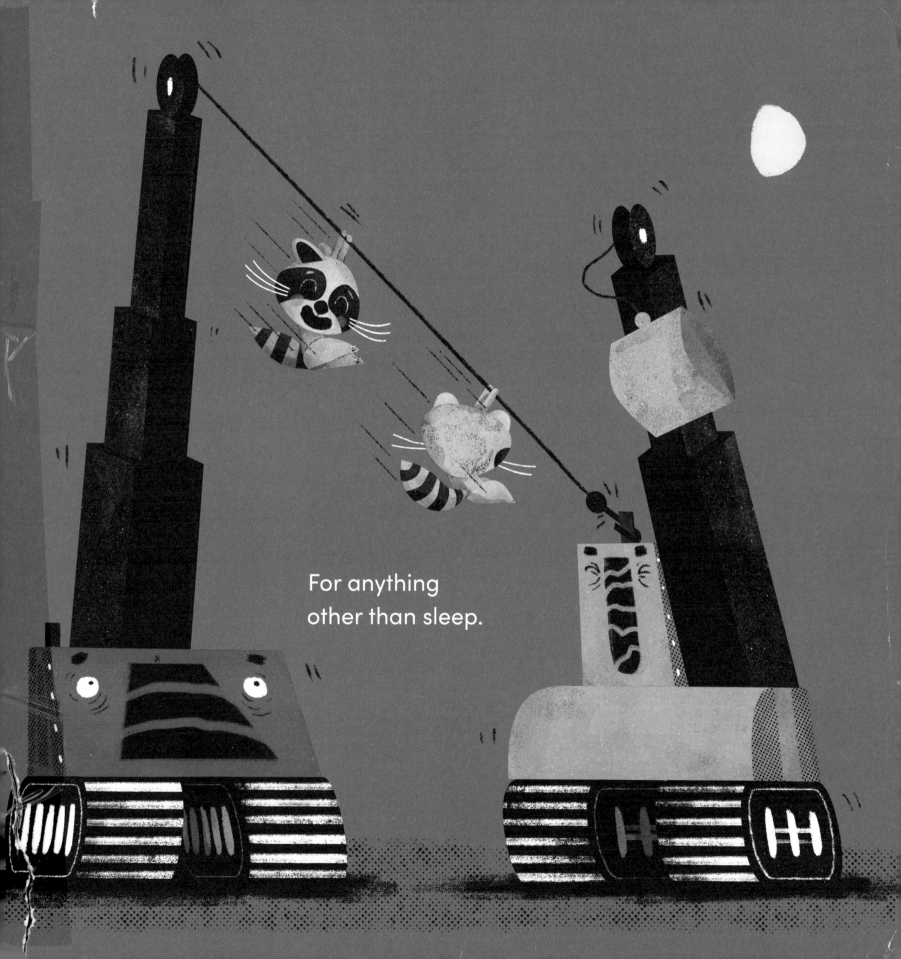

For anything
other than sleep.

Every morning, the big trucks went back to work.

"Are we done yet?" asked Crane.
"We need rest," said Stripes.

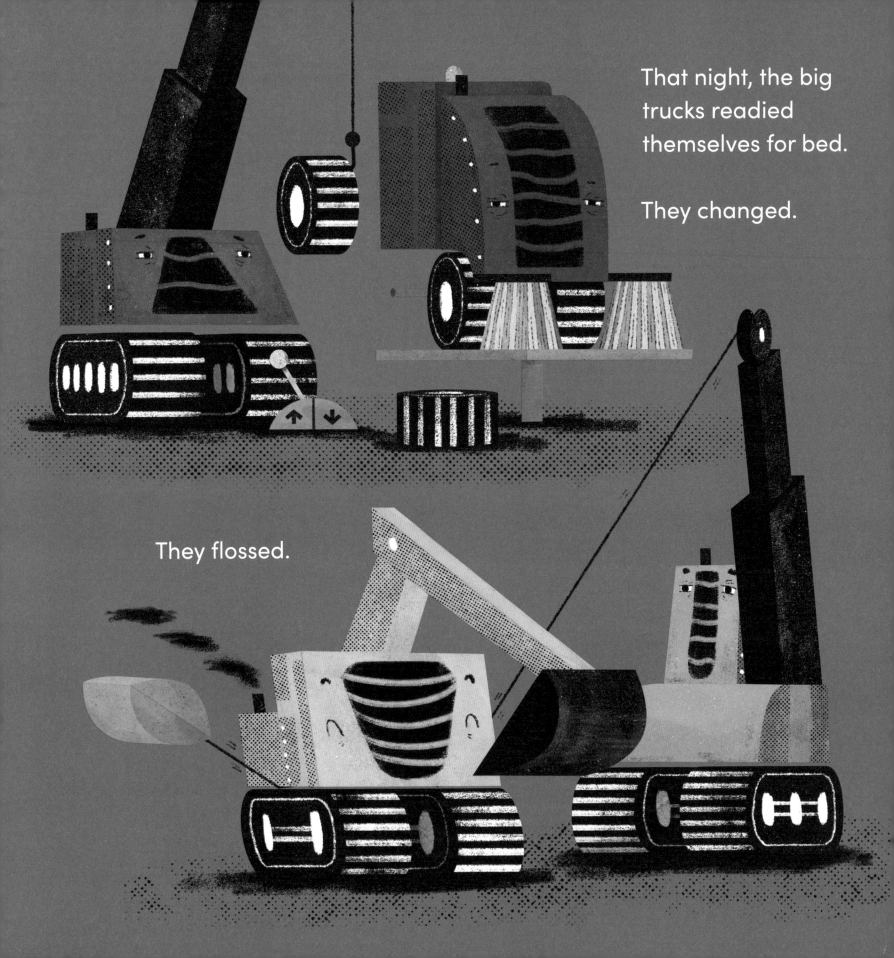

That night, the big trucks readied themselves for bed.

They changed.

They flossed.

They yawned.

The big trucks were beat.

By the time the raccoons returned . . .

everyone was asleep.

Everyone except for Digger.
But Digger was delirious.

"I am ready to play!" said
Digger. "I am wide awake."

The raccoons had other ideas.

The raccoons scurried up the slide.

They climbed the poles
and grabbed the flags.

They raced back to Digger . . .

"I am going to rest my eyes . . . ," said Digger.

The raccoons tucked Digger in
and gave him a kiss.

"Just for a minute . . . ," he said.

"Goodnight," said Digger.
"Squeak squeak," said the raccoons.

The raccoons sang Digger a bedtime song.

At last, beneath the light of the moon . . .

Digger and the big trucks dreamed.